PARKER'S SLUMBER PARTY

by **Parker Curry & Jessica Curry**
illustrated by **Brittany Jackson & Tajaé Keith**

Ready-to-Read

Simon Spotlight

New York   London   Toronto   Sydney   New Delhi

For my bestie, Gia, in memory of all the
slumber parties we've ever had together!
—P. C.

For my best friend, RGMEC—
I was not asleep, I was resting my eyes!
—J. C.

SIMON SPOTLIGHT
An imprint of Simon & Schuster Children's Publishing Division
1230 Avenue of the Americas, New York, New York 10020
This Simon Spotlight edition August 2024
Text copyright © 2024 by Parker Curry and Jessica Curry
Illustrations copyright © 2024 by Brittany Jackson
All rights reserved, including the right of reproduction in whole or in part in any form.
SIMON SPOTLIGHT, READY-TO-READ, and colophon
are registered trademarks of Simon & Schuster, LLC.
Simon & Schuster: Celebrating 100 Years of Publishing in 2024
For information about special discounts for bulk purchases, please contact
Simon & Schuster Special Sales at 1-866-506-1949 or business@simonandschuster.com.
The Simon & Schuster Speakers Bureau can bring authors to your live event.
For more information or to book an event contact the Simon & Schuster Speakers Bureau
at 1-866-248-3049 or visit our website at www.simonspeakers.com.
Manufactured in the United States of America 0724 LAK
2 4 6 8 10 9 7 5 3 1
CIP data for this book is available from the Library of Congress.
ISBN 978-1-6659-4279-9 (hc)
ISBN 978-1-6659-4278-2 (pbk)
ISBN 978-1-6659-4280-5 (ebook)

My name is Parker.
I am having
a slumber party tonight!

Mom helps me decorate,
plan games,
and pick the perfect snacks.

My new friends, Nora and Isabella, arrive first.

The doorbell rings.
It is my surprise guest, Gia!
I introduce my bestie
to my new friends.

"Nice to meet you,"
says Gia.

"Hi, Gia!" says Nora.
"We will have so much fun tonight," says Isabella.

Mom puts out the snacks.
"Yum! Gummy worms!"
Ava cheers.

We make friendship bracelets.
I make a bracelet for each
one of my friends.

Next we play board games and build a pillow fort. "Parker, the pizza is here!" Ava calls.

We eat pizza
and have cupcakes
with sprinkles for dessert.

Outside the sun sinks lower. We play flashlight tag until Mom calls us in.

Soon we are in our pajamas, but no one is tired.
We are having too much fun.

We use my flashlights to make shadow puppets on the wall.

"What is that?" Isabella asks.

"A little bird who will chirp the whole night," I whisper. "Then we can stay awake!" Gia and Nora giggle.

But Isabella and Ava
soon fall asleep.
After a while,
Nora starts to snore.
Then Gia drifts off.

I close my eyes for a minute.

When I open them,
it is morning!

We did not stay up all night, but we sure had fun trying!

FUN WITH FRIENDS

Parker loves spending time with her friends at slumber parties, playdates, and school. They have fun playing games and doing activities together. At the slumber party in this story, Parker and her friends played board games and flashlight tag, built a pillow fort, made friendship bracelets, and even created shadow puppets with their hands once the lights were out. Do you like any of the things that Parker and her friends did in this story? Are there other games and activities you and your friends love?

Have you ever had a slumber party with some of your friends? What games and activities would you plan for your slumber party? Do you think you would try to stay up all night?